No More Happy Endings

Milan Djurasovic

Červená Barva Press
Somerville, Massachusetts

Červená Barva Press
P.O. Box 440357
W. Somerville, MA 02144-3222

www.cervenabarvapress.com

Bookstore: www.thelostbookshelf.com

Cover Design: Aleksandra Djurasovic

ISBN: 978-0-9966894-8-9

ACKNOWLEDGMENTS

I would like to thank my wife, Anastasia Geinrikh, for her sweet love, humility and selflessness. I am forever grateful to my sister Aleksandra for her unconditional positive regard as well as my mother Jasna for her cuteness. I would also like to thank my best and main man Nikola Cubrilo and his family for bringing the familiarity of home to California for all these years. I must thank my good friend Eva Schepeler and Professor Demidova Olga for their advice and encouragement. Thanks go out to people I frequently think about: Bogdan, Aleksey, Jovica, Gulia, Graham, Catalin, Chatlin, Mathu, Michael, Kristina, Vova, Marina, and the kids from room nine at Aldar Academy. Last, I must thank my editor, Gloria Mindock, for her efforts to shed light on the little-known authors—or better still, for recognizing the light in their writing.

TABLE OF CONTENTS

BOSNIAN LULLABY   3

FANTASIES ARE FOR THE WEAK [OR,   5
WATCHING TELENOVELAS IN BOSNIA]

NEO-PLUMISM   8

GREEDY FOR CHICKEN LIVER PATE   10

POTATO BUG PRIORITIES   13

SMOKED HAM IS NOT ALL IT'S CRACKED   15
OUT TO BE

WHY WE STOPPED ATTACKING THE   20
ROMANI

A REPRESSED WIDOW   23

BRAS AND POTATOES   26

AN EXTRAORDINARILY SAD DAY   31

This book is dedicated to my grandparents Lazar and Jela Janjic, and to the gang of my childhood friends from Gacko.

No More Happy Endings

A BOSNIAN LULLABY

(1)

The bedtime stories of my grandmother, Baba Jela, changed after the Bosnian civil war. Before the shooting began, her stories were ordinary, positive, life-affirming, with a clever hero or good-natured idiot overcoming challenges and a greedy foe soon reduced to pitiful scrub. At the end, the world would turn out rosy and just, and taking part in it made sense. But after a war of nearly 100,000 deaths, millions of displaced bodies and souls, and decay peering out of every crack, such propriety seemed unnatural. So Baba Jela decided to get rid of it. While other elderly men and women decided to either withdraw into their private worlds or end their lives after realizing that nothing would ever again be the way it was before the war, Baba turned her stories and lullabies dark and horrifying, her own way of refusing to play along with uncontrollable circumstances.

The very first time I heard Baba Jela utter something that she wasn't supposed to say was during the bus ride that took us away from mutilated Mostar, our native town in Bosnia that to this day remains shattered. At the time I was only five years old, too young to realize that leaving one's house, a jailed husband, a missing son, 63 years of conducting one's life in a particular way, and a garden full of plants and flowers, especially her hybrid tea rose bushes which had started to bloom at the same time the foundation for the family house was laid out in 1961, could fill Baba's heart with so much boiling spite. Her mind was so clouded with tormenting resentment that she deliberately chose to hand over bits of her gloom to everyone around her. Baba Jela didn't spare anyone, not even her grandchildren.

The bus stopped in the sunny town of Stolac, famous for its speedy Bregava river and many kinds of songbirds. Unfortunately, none of us saw any of them because, together with about twenty other Serbs of different ages and vitalities, we were sitting in a grubby bus, waiting five hours to be exchanged for a handful of Croatian prisoners. After drawing a battlefield in a dusty window with my index finger brought on a sneezing fit, I decided to look for entertainment elsewhere. I walked over to where Baba Jela was sitting and asked her to tell me a story. Baba reluctantly agreed and then warned me that I wasn't going to like what I was about to hear. Dismissing her warning as a joke, I listlessly nodded my head and Baba began:

"Grandmother wants to sow flour
But her flour a dog devoured.

Where did the dog stray?
It disappeared in the hay.

Where is the hay now?
It's in the belly of our biggest cow.

Where has the cow gone?
Our people ate it before the dawn.

Where do our people hide?
In their graves because they all have DIED!"

Baba's thin lips jerked and tightened with every bitter word that came out of her mouth. The way she stressed the last line of the poem would have given heart tremors to Gautama Buddha. And the stomps of her feet made me run back to my mother's lap.

FANTASIES ARE FOR THE WEAK [OR, WATCHING TELENOVELAS IN BOSNIA]

In a poor part of a city,
A rich man does not linger,
Unless he strayed off his path,
Or has heard of a bosomy folk singer.

In a poor part of a city,
A rich man will acknowledge your existence,
Only if you can kick a football well,
Or if he is in need of some depraved assistance.

In a poor part of a city,
A rich man will shake your hand,
If you have long legs and a pretty face,
Or if he needs a drudge to tend his land.

For all the other reasons,
Rich man stays with rich,
So if you see him smiling at you,
He wants you to become his bitch.

It was impossible for my poor mother to indulge in fantasies for more than a couple of seconds at a time. If her thin and almost translucent lips stretched in a smile for too long, some kind of self-destructive instinct would shove her pitilessly back into harsh reality. And mother made sure to yank the others around her from their self-serving delusions, too, which made her a dreaded guest during the neighborhood's daily telenovela gatherings and discussions.

Escapism was as necessary as air and water after the war in Bosnia. People's worlds had not just been turned upside down, but tossed and kicked, spun and rolled, hurled towards an uncharted region. To forget about the two constants in their lives, fear and hopelessness, grownups drank a lot of alcohol, listened to a lot of turbo-folk, and sought comfort in the age-old truths and categorical justice of Latin working-class melodramas which inundated Balkan television sets during the 1990s.

Five families in our neighborhood chipped in to purchase a 12-inch, black and white television on which we could watch Kassandra, a telenovela about how true love between a gypsy maiden and her handsome beloved Luis David prevailed over Luis David's greedy twin brother Ignacio's and his evil stepmother Herminia's plans to annihilate them.

Every afternoon at four o'clock, in the cold basement of our neighbor's house (where we kept our communal TV and the only space that could fit all eighteen of us), we would invariably assume the same positions: the elderly on chairs in the front row and children strewn on the freezing concrete floor, on all sides.

Afraid that we would be inadvertently kicked, stepped on or salivated upon during the suspenseful moments, each kid usually kept one eye on the screen and the other on our excitable and demonstrative elders. Their faces contorted with every scene and their eyes beseechingly followed Kassandra's every move; some of the more passionate watchers even cursed and threatened the evil characters, and warned our heroine whenever she found herself in peril.

Since what we watched was a pirated version of the show, one day Kassandra abruptly disappeared from our lives. Pitying, or perhaps even fearing what the wretched souls of a warn-torn country might do if their only daily hour of tranquility was yanked from them, the U.S. State Department intervened to restore the show by pleading Antonio Paez of Coral Pictures to donate all 150 episodes of Kassandra to one of the Bosnian TV channel. Antonio obliged and hundreds of thousands of people were appeased.

Mother was not. She looked disparagingly at all those who were captivated by telenovelas. She refused to accept the convenient half-answers to life's toughest questions that

Kassandra offered. Therefore, whenever she joined us in our neighbors' basement, mother would heckle the actors, sigh loudly, and laugh sarcastically to remind everyone that the justice meted out on TV would never happen in real life.

However, during one of the last episodes of the series, as mother clapped her hands and covered her mouth in disbelief that we could drink in such nonsense, an older woman who lived in a small house down the street, gave her a reproachful look and said: "We know it's fake. Just leave us alone already." Mother shrugged her shoulders and watched the rest of the episode in silence.

NEO-PLUMISM

Some of us are young and some of us are old,
Naked in the snow we all feel cold.

Some like salty foods and others like theirs bland,
Smiling is unavoidable with a piece of chocolate in one's hand.

Some belong to this and some belong to that group,
After two plates of bean soup most of us will poop.

The majority of the herd is white but a few are black sheep,
When a disease kills a lamb both black and white weep.

Some are short as mushrooms and others are of massive height,
When someone says 'boo' we all jump in fright.

Some are smart and some are dumb,
The former read books while the latter fight over plums.

Despite total neglect, one pear and three plum trees in our front yard produced an abundance of delicious fruit. With four families living in our house, it was decided that each would claim one tree. But which would go to whom? The difference in the size of the trees and the amount of fruit they bore was significant, and we had a problem on our hands.

The four families gathered in the front yard under the canopy of the smallest plum tree to discuss dividing the fruit. Perhaps because he was the strongest and tallest among us, a man named Manojlo appointed himself the arbitrator of the plum tree partition.

"The smallest plum tree goes to you and your boys, Darinka," Manojlo said, turning his gaze towards the newest residents of our house. Darinka was a slender woman with ruddy, slightly saggy cheeks and a chest that was always congested with mucus. The index finger on her left hand was missing, and so was her husband Milan. But neither loss prevented

Darinka from getting up at four in the morning to walk four kilometers to the dairy farm, where she hand-milked forty cow udders, each and every day. "Ten minutes per cow," Darinka bragged whenever she was asked how she got everything done in a very short amount of time. "The secret is to sing to the cows and kiss their bellies as you milk them. If you do that, the milk will shoot out faster than water out of a nicked water pipe."

Darinka usually returned home at six o'clock in the evening with rough calluses on her nine swollen fingers, and was welcomed with a hot plate of soup and a spotless home that her two boys managed while she worked. (It is important to mention here that their home was a mouse-infested basement, which had only been cleared out and repainted by grandfather when this hardworking woman with ruddy cheeks knocked on our door asking for a scrap of bread to feed her two sons).

"I get the biggest plum tree because I have three adults and two ravenous children to feed," Manojlo said and looked around to see if anyone objected. No one dared to protest. His fist was the size of grandfather's head.

"Savo and his family get the pear tree because he is allergic to plums," continued Manojlo. "He can't even peel one without getting a rash and watery eyes. However, he will, and must, give each of us three jars of jam when his wife cooks it."

"I know that your family has the most members," Manojlo turned his eyes towards my grandfather, "but you'll have to accept the second biggest plum tree because your wife is Croatian." No other explanation was given.

"Grandma is Croatian?" I whispered to my mother, pulling on her sleeve. Both mother and grandmother were too scared to say anything. "How can grandma be our enemy?" I thought to myself.

That evening, I went to bed worried and confused. I could not believe that grandma was not one of us.

GREEDY FOR CHICKEN LIVER PATE

Five sisters lived in one house
All but one was meeker than a mouse
Together they worked, and together they played
And everything they had, four of them shared

One of them was selfish, she wasn't nice
And for her greed she paid a price

Five chicken eggs on one occasion she found
Without telling her sisters all five she swiftly downed

So long as her belly was allayed and replete
She didn't care that her sisters had nothing to eat
So listen up carefully and don't be surprised
When you hear of the punishment that God for her devised

Not so long after her stomach started to ache
She realized that her selfishness was a mistake
Her prayers and her remorse will no longer avail
Because a hatching chick her liver will soon impale

Through the girl's bellybutton the chick will appear
For the sister they'll cry but for the meat they'll cheer.

In April 1993, the small southeastern Herzegovinian town of Gacko became our new home. My grandfather was transferred to this cold and mountainous place after six months of torture in "Celovina" prison camp, where hundreds of Mostar Serbs, both men and women, had been held captive and beaten to a pulp. Along with two other Serb civilian prisoners, Bojan and Savo, my grandfather stumbled upon an empty house whose owner (a Bosnian Muslim) who, fearing for his life, abandoned his home in Gacko and, just like my grandfather, found a place with suitable ethnic and religious homogeny to continue existing.

Bojan, Savo and my grandfather converted two rooms of the abandoned house into a livable dwelling and took shelter there, cooking grass and snacking on tree bark, before their families joined them and crammed the space that already felt tight and oppressive. The living arrangement was at first comforting: snores, burps, farts, sweat, and stickiness became cherished reminders that we were still alive and breathing. Unfortunately, in such close proximity and intimacy with other hungry and bone-weary people, one quickly sees the worst side of humanity.

All but two members of our new household ate a plate of purified onion soup on the night of our arrival to Gacko. In addition to the soup, Bojan's two teenage sons ate a slice of bread each, covered with a thin layer of chicken liver pate. To this day I have never wanted to taste anything more than that oily mixture of chicken deliciousness. I even had a dream about it the following night, and woke up with a vinegary palate and a sour taste of disappointment, the following morning.

Bojan's wife Sanja noticed my salivating mouth and starved eyes, and she promptly informed us that she would have offered some pate to us if it hadn't been the last and only can of chicken pate in the house. My mother languidly shrugged her shoulders, I felt an awful urge to weep, and grandmother arched her hairless left eyebrow in suspicion, but no one said anything.

In the following months, all of our meals consisted of either purified onion soup or a slice of burnt bread with a chunk of cheese. In addition to hunger, our cramped living space became a big problem for the women of the house who were tired of wrapping blankets around their bodies every time they needed to put on clean clothes. Since there was another empty room on the same floor (it needed to be on the same floor because there was only one wood burning stove for all of us) we decided to make use of it. Armed with a broom, I joined my mother, grandmother and Sanja as they swept the disintegrating plank floor and scrubbed the damaged walls of what would become Bojan's family's bedroom. The only furniture left in the room was a dingy armchair and a dusty picture of former Yugoslavian socialist leader Josip Broz Tito. After about an hour of scrubbing and sweeping, a moment of terrible misfortune occurred. As grandmother tried to move the armchair so that she could sweep under it, something hard hit the floor.

"Don't move the chair!" Sanja shouted, but it was too late. Three cans of chicken liver pate had already slid from under the armchair cushion and landed in front of grandmother's feet.

The secret of why our family members were losing weight so much faster than Sanja and her boys was finally revealed. Sanja quickly bent over, picked up a can and extended it in grandmother's direction while grabbing her wrist with the other hand.

"Take it," she told the old woman who folded her arms and heartlessly whipped her with a sideways gaze that Clint Eastwood could learn plenty from. Grandmother sighed and shook her head for a moment before walking out of the room. Later that day grandma told my mother that Sanja's hand felt icy, like the hand of a dead woman.

POTATO BUG PRIORITIES

Boys, you have three choices
But the solution must be found without raising your voices
The first option is for one of you to withdraw
But it must be done without tears and a shivering jaw
The second option is to set it free
But with this decision the two of you will not agree
The third option will make both of you cry
To teach you a lesson this bug must die.

No one had any toys after the war. This was how almost all boys and girls in the small rural Herzegovinian town of Gacko became able to juggle four or more of whatever fruit or vegetable they had stolen from the townsfolk's orchards and vegetable gardens that particular day. Handling two plumbs in one hand was a piece of cake for most of us, and it was much harder to digest three raw bell peppers than to juggle them while blindfolded. Tarzan would have blushed with embarrassment if he had witnessed the speed and adroitness with which Gacko's boys and girls climbed trees and jumped from the balcony of one abandoned house to the forsaken front yard of another.

We captured frogs and insects and made them race inside a racetrack made out of empty milk cartons and around obstacles made out of empty cans of chicken liver pate. Once we even opened and successfully ran a zoo for over a week: there was a two-tailed lizard, a dozen frogs, a water snake, a wall-eyed kitten, and a three-legged dog. There weren't any toys to play with in early 1990's Bosnia, but there was plenty to do and think about.

My first friend in Gacko was another immigrant boy. His name was Dejan. Just like me, Dejan had lost his father in the war, but unlike mine, his father was a brave soldier who died in combat. My father didn't have a uniform or a gun, not even an army knife. When the five men in ski masks came to abduct him from our apartment, he was so scared that he peed himself. I, of course, hid this fact from my new friend. What I told him was that my father, whose biceps and martial arts expertise were bigger and better than Jean-Claude Van Damme's, and who was also a heavyweight boxing champion and a racecar driver before the war, had been captured by ten Croatian soldiers, seven of which he was able to eliminate with a variety of kicks and karate chops before the eighth coward snuck up behind him and cut him with a sword.

Dejan and I had many disputes over whose dad was braver and stronger, but our very first quarrel was not about the heroism of our fathers. It was about a potato beetle that we had found during one of our looting expeditions in a neighbor's vegetable garden. We made it fight against ants and race against a ladybug. When it was time for us to go home, we weren't able to decide which one of us was the rightful owner of the slimy creature.

Dejan's uncle Bajko called for us as soon as our bickering reached his ears and asked us to explain what the fuss was about. We hesitantly handed the beetle to him and for a moment he observed it as it walked across his hand. Bajko then extended his palm to us and showed us the potato beetle one last time before he slammed his other hand on top of it, flattening the little creature and staining his fingers with its insides. "Now go outside and think about whether you have something smarter to quibble about," Bajko commanded and gave us an angry look.

SMOKED HAM IS NOT ALL IT'S CRACKED OUT TO BE

He thought he was the top dog,
He thought he was the best,
He never hesitated to slog and flog,
He kept them all oppressed.

He had more than ten spouses,
He thought they were senseless,
He had more than ten houses,
He left none of them fenceless.

He paid one hundred for his shoes,
He paid his workers five,
He scorned and laughed at their blues,
He was the proudest man alive.

He didn't know that others had pride,
He didn't know they would resist,
He thought they would forever abide,
He was surprised by a powerful fist.

He destroyed countless lives,
He deprived men of their honor,
He was stabbed with countless knives,
He is now a goner.

He almost made me cry the first time I put on the purple winter jacket and purple rubber boots my mother had brought home from the Red Cross warehouse.

"You look really manly in purple," he told me through obnoxious laughter. Worst of all were the restrained but nevertheless noticeable and demeaning smiles on the faces of Perica's exclusively blond groupies.

Even prior to their mocking, my head had started spinning and my cheeks blushing when I spotted about a hundred other immigrant boys and girls in the school yard wearing the same purple winter jacket and purple rubber boots. I wanted to get rid of my clothes, cut them with scissors into small pieces and eat them…or throw them into a dumpster. But knowing how effortlessly my lungs attracted pneumonia and how furious my mother would be upon finding out that I had gotten rid of the only warm winter clothing she was able to get her hands on, I kept my purple garb and pretended, quite convincingly I may add, to like it in front of Perica and his ardent admirers.

Perica came from a wealthy local family. The first post civil-war boutique in the small Herzegovinian town of Gacko was opened and owned by his parents. While all the other mothers were elbowing and arguing with each other in waiting lines for food and clothes in front of the Red Cross warehouse, Perica's mother hired a professional tailor to make a coat and fitted jeans for her only child. From head to toe, everything Perica put on his lean and unnaturally muscular body was either custom-made or branded. Whenever he wore his long black cashmere coat and the original Dr. Martens cherry red boots on his feet, I was reminded of why he was so popular.

There were other reasons why I utterly despised Perica. He was the only boy in the whole neighborhood who owned a proper football and basketball, and that meant that he was the one who decided when, how, and with whom the rest of us were going to play. Perica usually selected the best players for his team and never felt a scrap of compunction when his team destroyed the opposition. After the game, the golden-haired cheerleaders hugged and congratulated their common heartthrob, telling him, depending on which sport we played, that he reminded them either of Zinedine Zidane or Michael Jordan.

"How can he look like both of them when one has white and the other black skin?" I would irritably inquire.

"You are just jealous," they would reply in unison.

And it was the rich and snooty Perica who forever ruined the game of tag for me. His blondies were designated chasers and they only ran after Perica while the rest of us stood in place and thought that chopping wood or even milking cows was far more entertaining than this fixed game.

"It'd be much easier to catch Svetozar," I would suggest every now and then. "He is fat and slow. That's the point of the game after all—to actually catch someone."

"You are just jealous we are not chasing you," the blondies would reply.

"I might be fat and slow but at least my nose isn't the size of a squash," angry Svetozar would say and punch me in the shoulder.

But the main reason why I hated Perica wasn't his sports equipment, expensive clothes or his popularity. I hated him the most because of the yummy food he flaunted in front of our starved eyes. While most of us ate sandwiches made of cheap spam, and if lucky, thinly sliced "slanina" (high-fat bacon), Perica's bakery roll was generally stuffed with mustard, enough trappist cheese to make three sandwiches for three hungry adults, and real smoked ham.

A week before the start of 1996 school year, the neighborhood boys had gathered in the school's yard to discuss the upcoming 'Back to School' football tournament. As Perica walked through the entrance gate, wearing brand new Reebok shoes and followed by his tattered blond-haired herd, Perica was munching a freshly made sandwich and drinking a can of Pepsi.

I was biting into and struggling to chew the burnt crust of my mother's homemade bread. Mother baked our daily bread in a cheap metal pan which usually caused the sides and the bottom of the loaf to burn while the interior remained damp and soft.

"That crust looks delicious," Perica said and giggled. "Chew it carefully or you'll break your teeth."

All the boys around us kept laughing for a long time even though most of their diets were identical to mine. Furthermore, they all knew that, just like me, they, or something they wore or ate or were related to, could at any moment become an object of Perica's derision. But that didn't stop them from deriving pleasure out of other people's misery and hoping that they could become good friends with Perica so they could enjoy the crumbs of his sandwiches and hand-me-downs he no longer wanted to wear.

"It usually isn't this burnt," was all I managed to say, referring to the crust. I wish that I had said nothing at all.

Just as the laughter subsided, our head teacher Borika Mijanovic appeared out of nowhere. She approached us with ginger steps and a friendly smile on her face.

"How are your parents?" she asked Perica, but before he was able to answer, Mrs. Mijanovic leaped like a professional male ballet dancer and slapped the sandwich out of Perica's hands. He fumbled it for a moment, but his shiny, crispy and crackling crusty bread was all he was able to save. Two thick slices of smoked ham and an even thicker slice of cheese were now lying beside his feet, covered in dirt.

"Out of my sight!" the teacher blustered with a voice of an angry giant looking for something to eat.

Perica looked at her in sheer disbelief for more than ten unbearably long seconds. He then turned around and walked away quietly while rubbing his tearful eyes. His gang of blond girls followed him shortly after.

When everyone, including Mrs. Mijanovic, walked away, I picked up the piece of ham that was still lying in dirt, blew on it and wiped with a sleeve of my shirt, and took a big bite out of it. This was the first time I tasted smoked ham and it is how I discovered, and to this day I still hold the same belief, that smoked ham is not all it's cracked out to be.

WHY WE STOPPED ATTACKING THE ROMANI

Both Ivan and Goran were flung into this world,
Ivan's was a smooth birth but Goran's was knurled.
Once out of his mother, Ivan was wrapped in silk,
To feed her Goran his mama was forced to bilk.

For Ivan's fifth birthday his dad gave him a beautiful puzzle,
For Goran's fifth birthday his dad handed him a beer to guzzle.
At the age of seven Ivan read his first grownup book,
A year later his mama's lifeless body Goran had to unhook.

By his fifteenth birthday Ivan had learned English and French,
From his fifteenth to sixteenth Goran sat on a prison bench.
Already at twenty three Ivan was happily married,
On his twenty fourth birthday next to his mama Goran was buried.

If you can't help the poor leave them alone,
They have enough problems on their own.

They moved into a roofless shack in May of 1996 and lived there for two weeks before anyone in our neighborhood noticed them. They were a family of gypsies, a well-regarded one before the war according to my grandfather Lazar, looking for a safe place to rest their weary heads. When, after walking for months through fields and forests, they stumbled upon an abandoned wooden hut that leaked water and reeked of cow dung, Ciga Angad and his family were more than elated to make it their new home. However, had they been aware of the destructiveness of their new surroundings caused by the perpetual boredom and fear of their new neighbors, Ciga Angad would have dragged his family right through the small post-war Herzegovinian town they settled in without even stopping for a drink of water.

The father of the family, Ciga Angad, was a short but powerfully-built man whose legs were so crooked that they outlined a perfect oval when he stood still. He had another peculiarity, too, which as soon as it was seen by the neighborhood women, became the talk of entire town and all the surrounding villages.

Soon after they arrived, Ciga Angad built an outdoor shower for his family. Just like their home, this wooden structure was full of gaps and crevices through which all the neighborhood boys shamelessly gawked and all the housewives bashfully glanced whenever they happened to walk near it—and they happened to be near it a lot. Within hours after his first scrubbing, the entire town had heard about and was discussing the powers of Ciga Angad's magic wand.

The more religiously fervent men said that Ciga Angad's oversized equipment was a curse from God for not following the teachings of Orthodox Christianity. The more religiously fervent women disagreed, and said it was a blessing. The more lighthearted among us joked that our new neighbor never had to fear any leg injuries because he kept a spare one within easy reach. "No policeman would ever dare to arrest Angad," was the beginning of my mother's favorite Ciga Angad joke, "because they would fall into the deepest depression if they ever saw the size of his baton."

. . .

Every day for well over a month after the family's arrival, Ciga Angad's small wooden shack was surrounded by a gang of about 20 school-age boys who shouted obscenities and pulled cruel, dangerous pranks. We set so many water traps that after a week of scares, Ciga Angad was not able to walk properly for more than three or four steps without ducking in fear of getting soaked. We threw rocks, mud balls and eggs at our new neighbors and wrote on their threadbare clothes and shoes whenever they put them outside to dry.

"Death to Gypsies!" was our most popular chant. "Gypsies get out!" was written on a piece of paper that was stapled to the doors of Ciga Angad's shack. In big red letters, another graffiti on their home read: "Gypsies are an inferior race."

Ciga Angad's wife Goroganka, a five-foot walking skeleton with gentle brown eyes, took the abuse with a restraint of a nun. Every now and then she'd politely ask us to leave her family alone, but as soon as one of the bigger boys threatened her with clenched fists, she would retreat and sigh as if to say: "I never really expected you to understand."

Her husband was just as patient, and his repressed anger would erupt only when his children were taunted. Bitterly annoyed by the incessant name calling, cursing and threats, with a stick in his hand he would run out of his home grunting and frowning, ready for confrontation. But outside, he was inevitably met by a group of rowdy boys huddled together, most of them taller than him by a head and salivating at the prospect of a fight.

The tormenting lasted until a man who lost a leg and a part of his hand in a war zone moved into our neighborhood. Ciga Angad's son Mudra was initiated into our gang after helping us steal and hide the man's crutch—an act of boldness that probably saved his father's life.

A REPRESSED WIDOW

Light brown is the color of your cup
Release what's in your chest before you blow up.
In the middle I see an enormous bull
With fears and worries your mind is full.
Next to the handle there is a long spike
Feel free to shout and cry as much as you like.
In this corner I've detected some barbed wire
With it you have wrapped your main desire.
You are restive because here is a trail of ants
The only remedy for this malady is found in a man's pants.

To acquire fame and reputation as a Turkish coffee fortune teller one must possess good intuition, decent eyesight, a wide knowledge of symbolism, and the ability and willingness to scare the devil out of skeptical audience.

My grandmother met all these proficiency requirements, easy. Bored, workless, and irascible women of Gacko frequently visited grandma in the hopes that the slimy grounds in their coffee cups would coalesce into recognizable, chocolate-colored figures of flowers, kangaroos, camels, sheep, fish, the sun, or a musical note. According to my omniscient grandmother, these things promised happiness and good fortune. On the other hand, dreaded animals and objects included: bayonets, balloons, babies, birds, snakes, all types of insects, rocks and pebbles. Because they forebode misfortune, these symbols were usually met with gaping mouths and headshakes of disbelief.

There were also a lot of monkeys! On good hair days, when her bangs spread out evenly across her forehead and the puffiness in the back was just right, grandma would cheer up the members of her clique by telling them that the monkeys in their coffee cups were, in fact, handsome secret admirers. But on humid days, when her hair turned frizzy and jumbled, grandma would see evil monkeys sneering and laughing at the coffee drinker's looks or stupidity.

"You must finish your coffee in four gulps if you want your wishes to come true," grandma would say whenever she was annoyed with a guest and wanted her (most men were not interested in the future) to leave our home. Poor women would burn their tongues and throats because they truly believed that their wishes would go to waste if they didn't swill as fast as the old woman commanded.

"I see a giraffe in your cup," was a finding that expressed grandma's exasperation with the intruding neighbors. Grandma would look them straight in the eye and say: "Do I have to remind you of what it means to have a giraffe in your cup? It means that you need to keep your lips zipped and think carefully about what's going to come out of your mouth. If it's drivel, then misfortune will befall your every step, for an entire week. I don't make up the rules. I wasn't the one who put the giraffe in your cup."

Ljupka Markovic, a jobless, restless, and a hopeless widow who lived across the street from us, visited grandma three, sometimes four times a week. As soon as she found out about her husband's death, Ljupka took to her balcony to publicly swear to herself, and to all the accidental passersby, that she would never marry again. Though Ljupka stayed true to her word, she often came to grandma with a collection of unwashed coffee cups, secretly wishing and hoping that the fortune-teller would spot a gondola, a water anchor, a palm tree, a parasol, or if she was really lucky, a racing horse right in the middle of her cup. All of these symbols promised success in love. When in a good mood, grandma easily spotted plenty of love symbols that turned Ljupka's cheeks red and warm. "Forget about love," Ljupka would say, blushing and smiling, "I want to know if I'll ever find some kind of work in this hellhole."

But on one humid August day, grandma woke up with especially frizzy and tangled hair. This meant that all propriety was thrown out of the window until humidity levels agreed with her desired hairstyle, or at least until a better quality hair comb was purchased. Unaware of the embarrassment that awaited her at our house, Ljupka and a friend of hers knocked on our door before the sun had risen and forced grandma to cover her head with a shawl. After they drank their coffee, they politely asked grandma to take a look at their cups. Grandma took Ljupka's cup first and without much delay she said: "There is an enormous penis in the middle of your cup. You must be very horny."

Upon hearing grandma's words, Ljupka opened her eyes in a frenziedly tragic stare and said: "You old hag! I'll never come back here again." She staggered towards the entrance door and broke into sobs as her shoes eluded her feet. Ashamed and a little dizzy, Ljupka picked them up with her shaky hands and clambered out of the house barefoot.

Ljupka Markovic came back a week later holding two empty coffee cups in her hands. We all knew she was going to come back. There wasn't much else for a young widow to do in the small, rural, post-civil-war Bosnian town of Gacko. With tears in her eyes and cracks in her syllables, Ljupka recited a long apology and asked grandma to take a look at her cups because she had spotted a mouse in both of them and they worried her. Grandma accepted the apology with a gracious smile. That day, her hair was perfectly coiffed.

BRAS AND POTATOES

Go to hell you old cheat
Lewdness will be your defeat.
Since you chose that hoary witch
It must have been a serious itch.

My husband has lost his sense of shame
He sells bras and panties with an old dame.
To hundreds of women he now suggests
With what to cover their bare breasts.

My grandmother occasionally took care of my grandfather while they were growing up in what was then known as the Kingdom of Serbs, Croats and Slovenes. She was nine years older than him and this fact, which was well-known to everyone who visited our family in spite of our careful and thorough efforts to conceal it, caused grandma a lot of embarrassment.

"He was restive as a child," grandma would say whenever her husband wasn't around to take orders from her, "and sixty years later, he is still running around like a frantic chicken being chased by a butcher."

My grandfather's family called Raška Gora their home, a desolate and rocky village located some 35 kilometers from Mostar, which according to grandma, was populated only by lazy idiots and oversexed lunatics. Her village, a similarly forsaken and hilly terrain by the name of Goranci, was according to grandma's stories, a patch of land renown for the purity and nobleness of minds and spirits of its residents.

During World War II, grandma's four older brothers joined the German occupiers and two of them settled in Bavaria after the war ended. To this day, they, and their very large progeny, live and work in Munich, and they visit their

Bosnian relatives whenever their family vacations on the Adriatic. Her other two brothers were most likely killed in combat. Along with her four sisters, grandma spent her childhood doing the work that her brothers would have done had there not been a war.

On the other hand, a better part of grandfather's family was killed and dispersed, rendering him an orphan at the age of four (his father was killed by the Nazis and his mother fled, leaving her child behind). Grandpa was raised by his crazy uncle Jovan who beat and berated him for every little mistake he made as he ploughed the land, transplanted seedlings by hand, chopped wood, and looked after livestock.

"He returned to my village after the war with a thick mustache and tender red pimples all over his forehead," was how grandma usually started her story of how she finally gave in to grandfather's whimpers and beseeching to accept his marriage proposal.

"I had many offers. A river of men lined up to offer me a pampered life, but he just wouldn't go away. Day or night, rain or shine, sickness or vigor, he just wouldn't leave. My father Ivan, who wasn't fond of Serbs and used to call them Srbćici (tiny Serbs), threatened him with an ax, but he was more stubborn than a deaf mule. When I was a young woman we didn't have all the lipsticks and eyeliners and perfumes. We used burnt matches as pencils to make our eyes appear bigger; we stuffed crushed rose petals in our underwear, used a bit of rope to push up our breasts, and brushed our teeth with ash we collected after beating two stones together.

My grandparents married, worked, built their house, had three children (the youngest boy died after he accidently swallowed and choked on a handful of raw beans), and lived respectable lives in what was then known as The Socialist Federal Republic of Yugoslavia.

Bosnian Civil War had separated my grandparents once again. In summer of 1992, my grandfather was taken away by a group of Croatian soldiers and placed in a prison where he was again severely beaten and berated for every little mistake he made digging trenches near the front lines and cleaning soldier's boots and bathroom tiles with his tongue. Grandma was told that her husband was accused of receiving and transmitting radio signals to the Serb soldiers even though no equipment was ever found and grandfather's hearing had been severely impaired by the loud mining machinery he had worked with for three decades.

Grandma and grandpa were reunited in the summer of 1994 in what is now known as The Republika Srpska, one of two administrative entities in Bosnia and Herzegovina. Although they had never physically or verbally demonstrated how much they missed each other—mostly because they thought of hugging and kissing in front of other people to be indecent—it was obvious to everyone around them that they were overjoyed to be back together under the same roof.

More than two years passed since their reunion before they had their first quarrel, and it was a serious one.

One rainy April day, two weeks after the last spring frost, grandfather returned home after a long and tiring day of preparing the soil for potatoes. He washed his hands and face and then he sat down next to his wife to update her on what kind of seeds he was thinking of using.

As soon as he sat next to her, grandma turned her face in the opposite direction and silently muttered: "You are dead to me."

Grandfather's face acquired a pale yellowish tint. As he opened his mouth to ask for an explanation, grandma dismissed him with a swift wave of her bony arm.

The following day, after another grueling day of work in his vegetable garden, grandfather returned home with a bag of the local "Torotan" cheese. Smiling and giddy to share with his wife how cheaply he purchased the quality product he held in his hands, he sat down next to his wife who was in a middle of chewing a mouthful of baked potatoes. As soon as she swallowed and made sure that no crumbs lingered on her whiskers, grandma again turned her head away from her husband and said: "You are dead to me."

...

To make ends meet grandfather did all kinds of work. He cultivated any patch of land he was given by the locals, he loaded coal into other people's basements and fixed bicycles and umbrellas for half a kilogram of lard, and he helped elderly woman sell lingerie at the marketplace in exchange for a discount on felt boots and wool socks.

When Desanka, an eighty-year-old neighborhood informant, told grandma that her husband spends four hours every Friday holding women's undergarments in his hands, continuously shouting: "great quality bras for all sizes," her body shuddered and she nearly fainted from all the jealousy and humiliation. When she discovered that he was doing this in a partnership with another woman, grandma grated her teeth so hard that one of her molars cracked in half.

"You wouldn't be eating those potatoes and drinking that yogurt if it weren't for those bras," grandfather tried to explain and then quickly covered his head because a plate of boiled potatoes and yogurt was about to land on his face. The plate broke and cut the bottom of his chin. Potatoes and yogurt ended up in his lap.

This incident was the first and last time I had seen grandma refuse boiled potatoes with yogurt, and that same day grandfather regretfully left the ladies' undergarment business.

AN EXTRAORDINARILY SAD DAY

It was only two days before our departure for the United States of America that she disclosed the life-changing news to her family. Partly because she was afraid of the infectious chatter and slander that this event would bring about in our neighborhood, and partly because she was even more terrified of my grandmother's, Baba Jela's reaction, my mother Jasna had kept her lips zipped for three long months without revealing a slightest hint about a decision that was going to take us away to a completely new world.

"I just couldn't say no to his offer," said mama softly, nervously looking at Baba Jela's thin, knitted eyebrows. "Three meals a day with meat for lunch, good quality clothes and waterproof shoes for my children, and maybe even some kind of work for me; it's an opportunity I must take. I am aware that he is twenty years older and that he had been married twice before, but what was I supposed to say given that there is no hope for me and my little ones here?"

The next day, as we were stuffing our clothes and picture albums in our backpacks, it was still unclear to me what was going on. Baba Jela had not moved from her chair and she had not uttered a single word since mama had told her about some generous old man whose offer she wasn't able to refuse. For hours, Mama frantically ran around Baba Jela, futilely begging for eye contact and her blessing.

With our bags packed and stacked next to the entrance door, our family sat in the living room from six o'clock in the evening until midnight without anyone moving or saying anything.

Five minutes after midnight, right after Baba Jela's first yawn, staring blankly at the ground mama timidly whispered:

"You remember the advice you once gave me: to do anything, absolutely anything, for the betterment of my little ones?"

A moment later, when Baba Jela's red and teary eyes opened wide and peered at her, mama added: "Well, that is what I am doing."

Without the least hesitation, Baba Jela separated her thin, dry lips, unhurriedly moistened them with her narrow tongue and replied:

Grandma was too old and too sickly,
To get rid of her they decided quickly.
To let her die in her house she cried and pleaded,
But neither her mind nor her body was needed.

Her son Milan lifted her over his shoulder,
Sharp pity and bitter sorrow he tried to smolder.
He carried her across the field and into a dark thicket,
All they could hear was somber chirping of a cricket.

Milan lowered his mother on a cold wet rock,
She hugged him tightly and he heard her squawk:
'This same rock is where I left my own mother,
The guilt will kill you, don't commit the same blunder.'

Milan closed his eyes and plugged his ears with cotton,
He whispered that it wasn't him, that life was just so rotten.
Forty years have passed since then, and now it's Milan's turn,
To sternly warn and beg his own child his death to adjourn.

I cuddled up next to Baba Jela, but rather than looking at her swollen eyelids and hazy eyes of a tired puppy, and numerous red blotches which formed on her hollow cheeks whenever she cried, I turned my face toward the ant infested cracks of our living room walls. As I watched them run around, I remembered something I had read about these little creatures in my biology book - a fact which made me shudder all over with anxiety. This fact, which had affected me profoundly as soon as I read it, and which was now making my heart race across my chest and climb up into my throat, informed that a satiated ant regurgitates a drop of transparent fluid whenever it encounters a hungry comrade.

"While ants take care of each other," I thought to myself as I listened to sporadic grunts and irregular beating of Baba Jela's enfeebled heart, "we are leaving our grandmother to live out the rest of her days in heartache and loneliness."

That was the first time I had sincerely wished for death to come and alleviate the misery by taking away either me or my Baba Jela. My wish was not granted. Instead, we sat quietly for another three hours before everyone except mama, one by one, started to doze off.

Three hours later, mama gently shook my shoulders to let me know that it was time to go. My sister was already dressed in her nicest clothes and she sat next to grandfather Lazar, wiping his tears with her fingers and telling him that we were going to come back and visit the first chance we get. He covered his head with his forearms, embarrassed to be seen crying. Unlike Baba Jela, grandfather Lazar bowed to the inevitable.

When I got dressed, Baba Jela was still sleeping with her mouth slightly ajar. Her eyelids were moist and a tear dangled on the tip of her nose. I went toward her to wake her up but mama pulled me away and muttered that it would be better for all of us if we slip out unnoticed. But as we tried to get out, the old entrance door squeaked, and Baba Jela jumped up as if fired out of a pistol. After rubbing her gluey eyes, in a weak, raspy voice she said:

"I advise you not to go."

My mama, smothered in nerves and exhaustion, looked at her own mother, the woman with whom she spent every single day of her thirty five years, shrugged her shoulders and exhaled through tightly pressed lips, and, turning to my sister and me, said: "We'll be late if we don't get going."

ABOUT THE AUTHOR

Milan Djurasovic is a Bosnian Serb from Mostar, the descendant of delightful peasants and modest working-class stock. He lives in northern California, where he works as a paraeducator. *No More Happy Endings* is his first collection of poems and short stories.